SHEEP, SHEEP, SHEEP,
Help Me Fall Asleep

written and with photographs by ARLENE ALDA

A Picture Yearling Book

Published by
Bantam Doubleday Dell Books for Young Readers
a division of
Bantam Doubleday Dell Publishing Group, Inc.
1540 Broadway
New York, New York 10036

The trademark Yearling® is registered in the U.S. Patent and
Trademark Office.
The trademark Dell® is registered in the U.S. Patent and
Trademark Office.
ISBN: 0-440-40957-8
Reprinted by arrangement with Doubleday Books for Young Readers
Printed in the United States of America
April 1995

10   9   8   7   6   5   4   3   2

DAN

Designed by Jane Byers Bierhorst
Text set in 17 point ITC Berkeley Old Style Medium

To giggles and rhymes
And family times

With special thanks to
Tabatha, Briony, Joe Henson,
John Croft, and Paul Donohue of
the Windsor Safari Park,
England.

I couldn't fall asleep one night.
My mommy said, "That's quite all right.
Just close your eyes and look for sheep.
Then count them and you'll fall asleep."
I closed my eyes the way she said.
I didn't see the sheep; instead…

I saw a very itchy cow

A cat too busy to meow

And piglets in mud, which they liked, I suppose.

I saw those animals, none of them sheep—
Well, that seemed better than falling asleep.
I stretched and whispered, "Boy, this is fun.
Before I see sheep, the night will be done."
Then a fat hippo smiled. (I wondered what for.)

And a goat played peek-a-boo out her front door.

Some geese went out walking, all in a line.

A horse started talking. (His voice was like mine!)

I got awfully tired while looking for sheep,
But somehow or other, I still couldn't sleep.
I wiggled, I squirmed, I turned and I tossed.
Where were the sheep? Could they have been lost?

At last I saw one. It had wooly hair.

Then there were two of them. That made a pair.

I counted to three. I looked for some more.

My eyelids were heavy when there were four.

Five sheep. Now six.

Then seven

and eight.

Nine came along. I think it was late.

I yawned a big yawn and counted to ten.
There were too many sheep to start counting again.

I finally slept like a lamb — yes, that's true.

But oh how I wished for a big kangaroo!